An I Can Read Book®

A SYD HOFF TREASURY

Syd Hoff

Sammy the Seal

Stanley

Grizzwold

BARNES & NOBLE
BOOKS
NEW YORK

Reprinted by permission of HarperCollins Publishers

Library of Congress Catalog Card Number: 59-5316
ISBN 0-06-022525-4
ISBN 0-06-022526-2 (lib. bdg.)
ISBN 0-06-444028-1 (pbk.)

Sammy
THE SEAL

Story and pictures by **Syd Hoff**

HarperTrophy®
A Division of HarperCollins*Publishers*

It was feeding time at the zoo.

All the animals

were getting their food.

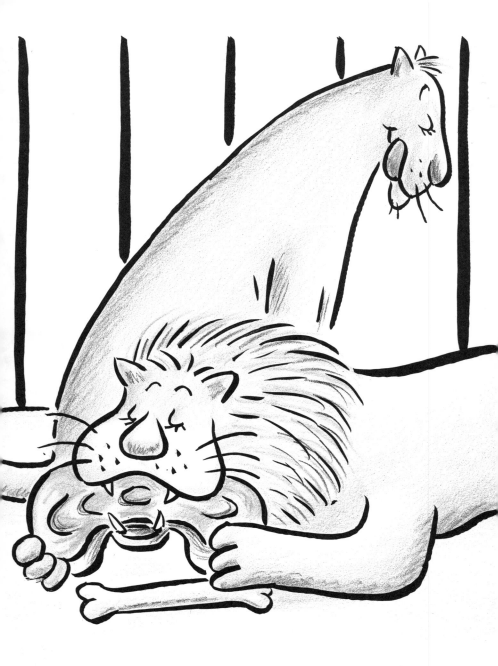

The lions ate their meat.

The elephants ate their hay.

The monkeys ate their bananas.

The bears ate their honey.

Then it was time

for the seals to be fed.

Mr. Johnson took them fish.

"Hooray for fish!" said the seals.

They jumped in the water.

Soon the basket was empty.

"That is all there is," said Mr. Johnson.

"There is no more."

"Thank you for the fish," said the seals.

"They were good."

The seals were happy.

But one little seal was not happy.

He sat by himself.

He looked sad.

"What is wrong, Sammy?"

said Mr. Johnson.

"I want to know

what it is like

outside the zoo," said the little seal.

"I want to go out and look around."

"All right, Sammy," said Mr. Johnson.
"You have been a good seal.
You may go out and see."

"Good-bye, Sammy," said the other seals.

"Have a good time."

"Good-bye," said Sammy.

"Where are you going?" said the zebra.

"I am going out," said Sammy.

"Have fun," said the hippo.

"Come back soon," said the giraffe.

Sammy walked and walked and walked.

He did not know what to look at first.

"That seal must be from out of town,"
said a man.

Sammy looked at everything.

"What street is this?" said a man.

"I am a stranger here myself,"

said Sammy.

"I guess it is feeding time here, too,"
said Sammy.

"That is a lovely fur coat," said a lady.

"Where did you get it?"

"I was born with it," said Sammy.

"I wish I could find some water.
I am hot. I want to go swimming,"
said Sammy.

"We are sorry. There is no room for you

in this puddle," said the birds.

"And there is no room for you here,"
said the goldfish.

"Keep out," said the policeman.

"You cannot swim in there."

"Ah, here is a place!" said Sammy.

"Who is in my bathtub?" said someone.

"I am sorry," said Sammy.

He left at once.

Some children were standing in line.

Sammy got in line, too.

"What are we waiting for?"

asked Sammy.

"School. What do you think?" said a boy.

"That will be fun.

I will come, too," Sammy said.

The teacher was not looking.

Sammy sat down.

The children made words with blocks.

Sammy wished he could spell.

"All right, children.

Now we will all sing a song,"

said the teacher.

The children had good voices.

"That sounds fine," said the teacher.
"But one of you is barking—
just like a seal."

"Is it you, Joey?"

said the teacher.

"No," said Joey.

44

"Is it you, Helen?"

said the teacher.

"No," said Helen.

45

"Is it you, Dorothy, Robert,

Fred, Joan, or Agnes?"

"No," said the children.

46

"Then it must be you,"
said the teacher.

"I am sorry. This school is just for boys and girls."

"Please let me stay," said Sammy.

"I will be good."

"All right. You may stay,"

said the teacher.

Sammy was happy.

He sat at his desk

and looked at the teacher.

He learned how to read.

He learned how to write.

"And now it is time to play,"

said the teacher.

"Who wants to play a game?"

"We do," said the children.

53

They threw the ball over the net.

"The ball must not hit the ground,"
cried Sammy's team.

"Somebody catch the ball."

Sammy caught the ball on his nose!

A boy on the other team tried
to catch the ball on his nose, too.
"Boys must catch with their hands,"
said the teacher.

Sammy tried to catch the ball
with his flippers.

"Seals must catch with their noses,"
said the teacher.

Up and down went the ball,

from one side to the other.

At last the teacher blew her whistle.

"Who wins?" said the children.

"It is even," said the teacher.

Everybody was happy.

A bell rang. School was over.

"Will you be here tomorrow?"
said the children.

"No," said Sammy.

"School is fun,

but I belong in the zoo.

I just wanted to know

what it is like outside.

Now I have to go back."

"Good-bye, Sammy," said the children.

"We will come to see you."

"Good," said Sammy.

Sammy was in a hurry

to get back to the zoo.

He had so much to tell the other seals.

"May I welcome you home, Sammy,"
said Mr. Johnson.

"I am glad you are back.

You are just in time for dinner."

"There's no place like home,"

said Sammy.

STANLEY

Other I CAN READ BOOKS® by Syd Hoff

Danny and the Dinosaur

Julius

Sammy the Seal

Oliver

Who Will Be My Friends?

Albert the Albatross

Chester

Little Chief

Grizzwold

The Horse in Harry's Room

Thunderhoof

Barkley

Santa's Moose

Barney's Horse

Mrs. Brice's Mice

An I Can Read Book®

STANLEY

Story and Pictures by

Syd Hoff

HarperTrophy®

A Division of HarperCollins*Publishers*

HarperCollins®, ✎®, Harper Trophy®, and I Can Read Book®
are trademarks of HarperCollins Publishers Inc.

Stanley
Copyright © 1962, 1992 by Syd Hoff
Printed in the U.S.A. All rights reserved.
Newly Illustrated Edition
Published in hardcover by HarperCollins Publishers.

Library of Congress Cataloging-in-Publication Data
Hoff, Syd, date
  Stanley / by Syd Hoff.
      p.   cm. — (An I can read book)
  Summary: Chased away by the other cavemen because he is different,
Stanley finds a new and better way of living.
  ISBN 0-06-444010-9 (pbk.)
  [1. Man, Prehistoric—Fiction.   2. Self-confidence—Fiction.]
I. Title.   II. Series.
PZ7.H672Ss   1992   91-12266
[E]—dc20   CIP
                                                                       AC

New Harper Trophy edition, 1992.

STANLEY

A long time ago there were no houses
and people lived in caves.

9

Stanley lived in a cave,

but he did not like it.

The cave was cold.

So Stanley was cold.

11

His head hurt because

he had to sleep with it on a rock.

12

Bats flew around as though

they owned the place.

"Why can't we find
a better way to live?"
asked Stanley.

"This is good enough for us,"

said the other cavemen.

"Why isn't it good enough for you?"

The cavemen carried clubs.

They were very tough.

16

Stanley was tough, too.

But he liked to plant seeds

in the ground

and watch them grow.

18

He liked to paint pictures.

19

He liked to be nice to people.

He was kind to animals.

The other cavemen did not
want Stanley to act this way.
"Can't you act more like a
caveman?" they asked.

Stanley did not answer.

He went on planting seeds

and painting pictures.

He went on being kind to animals
and nice to people.

He even started saying things like
"Please," and "Thank you,"
and "Lovely day today, isn't it?"

25

This made the other cavemen
very angry.

"You can't live here," they said.
"Beat it!"

They threw rocks at Stanley

and chased him away.

"We're sorry you lost your cave,"
said the animals.

"I don't care," said Stanley.

"It was cold anyway."

28

He looked for a place to live.

"You can't live in a nest,"

said the birds.

"You can't live in the water,"
said the fish.

"You can't live in the ground,"
said a worm.

"Maybe I can live in a tree,"
said Stanley.

"Not while I'm up here,"

said an ape.

33

"Maybe I can live in space,"

said Stanley.

He jumped off a rock.

"Ouch!" said Stanley.

"I can't live in space!"

35

Stanley saw a field.

"Does anybody mind if I live here?"
he asked.

"I don't mind if you don't snore,"

said an animal

who was going to sleep.

37

"I don't mind if you don't

eat too much grass,"

said an animal who was eating.

38

"I don't mind

if you don't take up

too much room,"

said a very,

very big animal.

Stanley made himself at home.

"This is not bad," he said.

But suddenly the wind blew

and Stanley was cold.

The rain fell and he was wet.

41

"This is worse than the cave,"

said Stanley.

He made walls

to keep out the wind.

42

He made a roof

to keep out the rain.

43

He made a door,

windows and chimney.

He made a house!

44

"That's the first house I ever saw,"
said a field mouse.

"It's the first one I ever made,"

said Stanley.

"Won't you stay here

and live with me?"

"I can't. I belong in the field.

But I will come and visit you

from time to time,"

said the field mouse.

47

Stanley painted pictures.

He planted seeds in the ground

and watched them grow.

49

He loved his house.

But he was lonesome.

"I wonder how my friends are,"

he said.

The cavemen were out

hunting for animals.

They carried their clubs.

"Look who's after us

with their silly clubs,"

said the animals.

"Let's chase them out of here!"

52

They chased the cavemen.

Stanley saw the cavemen running.

"Don't be afraid," he said.

"I won't let them hurt you."

He made the animals go away.

"You saved us, Stanley,"

said the cavemen.

"Thank you."

"Come back and live in our cave,"
said one caveman.

"Caves are old-fashioned," said Stanley.

"Come and see where I live."

He showed them his house.

"A cave is for bears.

A house is for people,"

said Stanley.

60

"You are right, Stanley,"

said the cavemen.

"This is the way we want to live."

They all made houses.

Stanley showed them

how to paint pictures

and plant seeds.

He showed them
how to be nice to each other
and kind to animals,
and everybody was happy.

Grizzwold

Story and pictures by
Syd Hoff

An I CAN READ Book

HarperTrophy®
A Division of HarperCollins*Publishers*

Library of Congress Catalog Card Number: 63-14366
ISBN 0-06-022480-0
ISBN 0-06-022481-9 (lib. bdg.)
ISBN 0-06-444057-5 (pbk.)
First Harper Trophy edition, 1984.

Grizzwold

In the far North

lived a bear named Grizzwold.

Grizzwold was so big

three rabbits could sit in his footprint.

When he went fishing,

the river only came to his knees.

Other bears had no trouble
going into caves to sleep.
Grizzwold always got stuck.

8

He had to sleep out in the open.

But he didn't mind.

He had a nice coat of fur

to keep him warm.

No other animal dared wake him.

10

One morning there was a loud noise

in the forest.

All the other bears ran away.

Grizzwold went to see what it was.

He saw men chopping down trees.

"Timber!" they shouted.

"What's the big idea?" asked Grizzwold.

"What are you doing to my forest?"

14

"We are sorry," said the men.

"We have to send these logs

down the river to the mill.

They will be made into paper."

"I can't live in a forest
with no trees," said Grizzwold.

16

He went to look

for a new place to live.

17

"Do you know

where there is a nice forest?"

he asked.

"You won't find one up here,"
said a mountain goat.

19

"Do you know

where there is a nice forest?"

he asked.

20

"You won't find one here,"
said a prairie wolf.

21

"Do you know

where there is a nice forest?"

he asked.

22

"Boy, are you lost!"

said a desert lizard.

Grizzwold looked until he saw houses.

"What can I do here?" he asked.

"You can be a bearskin rug,"
said some people.

26

They let him into their house.

Grizzwold lay down on the floor.

The people stepped all over him.

"Ow! I don't like this," said Grizzwold.

He left the house.

Grizzwold saw a light pole.

"I'll climb that tree," he said.

"I was here first," said a cat.

32

He chased Grizzwold away.

Grizzwold saw a dog.

"Can't you read?" asked the dog.

34

He chased Grizzwold away.

Grizzwold saw people going to a dance.

The people wore masks.

Grizzwold went to the dance too.

"You look just like a real bear,"
said the people.

"Thank you," said Grizzwold.

38

The people started to dance.

Grizzwold started to dance too.

"It is time to take off our masks,"
said somebody.

40

All the people took off their masks.

"Take off yours too,"

they said to Grizzwold.

"I can't," he said.

"This is my real face."

"You don't belong here,"

said the people.

"You belong in the zoo."

Grizzwold went to the zoo.

The bears were begging for peanuts.

Grizzwold begged too.

"Please don't stay," said the bears.

"We need all the peanuts we get.

Try the circus."

Grizzwold went to the circus.

They put skates on him.

He went FLOP!

50

They put him on a bicycle.

He went CRASH!

They tried to make him

stand on his head.

52

He couldn't do that either!

"I guess it takes practice,"

said Grizzwold.

"It sure does," said the trained bears.

Grizzwold tried to rest.

"You can't park here,"

said a policeman.

"I'll find a place to park,"

said Grizzwold.

He ran until he came to a nice forest.

"I'm very glad to be here," he said.

"We are very glad you are here too,"

said some hunters.

They took aim.

"Don't shoot!" said a ranger.

"This is a national park.

No hunting allowed."

59

The hunters left.

"Thank you," said Grizzwold.

60

"You will be safe here,"

said the ranger.

"People cannot shoot animals here.

They can only shoot pictures."

All the people

wanted to take Grizzwold's picture.

He was the biggest bear

they had ever seen.

"Thanks for posing for us,"

they said.

63

"This is the life for me,"

said Grizzwold.

He was very happy.

64